SPACEM
SPACEMF
and other rhymes

GW00854782

Barbara Ireson

Illustrated by Ann Axworthy

PICTURE CORGI

Spaceman, Spaceman

Spaceman, Spaceman take me, too.
Let me fly in space with you.
Let me come aboard today
So that we can zoom away.
Can we set a course for Mars ?
Can we blast off for the stars ?

All Ready

Checked—all the switches.
Checked—every light.
Temperature's normal.
Pressure's all right.
Ground control signals;
A message comes through,
'We're counting you down
So good luck to you.'

In Orbit

Round the Moon in orbit
My rocket has to go ;
Round and round and round
because
My crew is down below.

Six of them have landed,
They all have work to do,
It's lonely here without them
Just circling till they're
through.

Round the Moon in orbit
My rocket has to go ;
Round and round and round
because
My crew is down below.

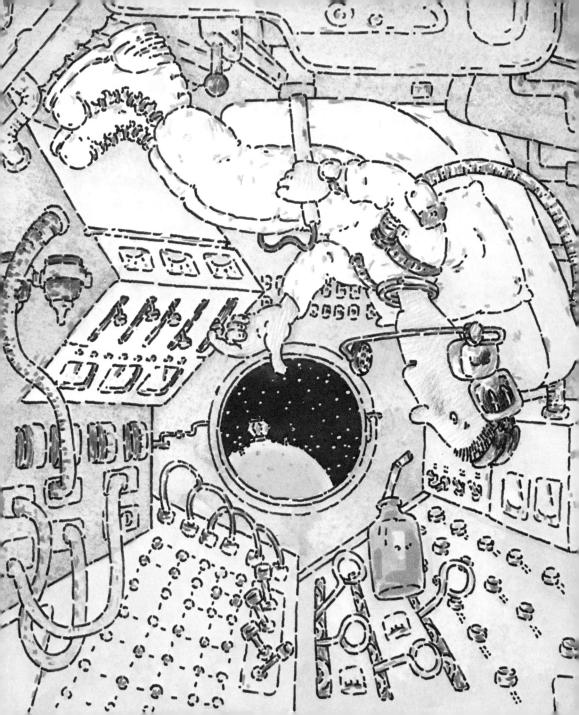

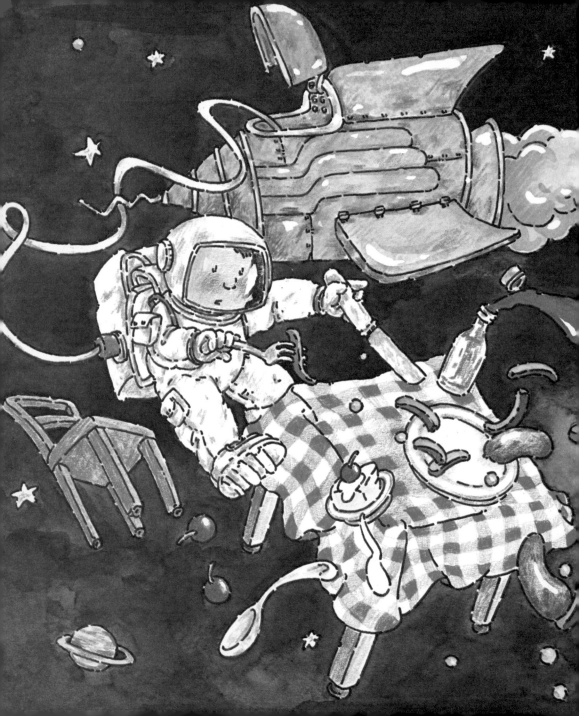

Spaceman's Complaint

It's very difficult for me,
When I'm in space, to eat
my tea.
I float about, I have no
weight
And keep on going past
my plate.

Star-trip

Where is it mermaids swim in the
sea ?
Where is it unicorns roam about
free ?
Is there a planet where dragons
are found
And witches on broomsticks still
hover around ?
Is there a planet where giants
and gnomes
And spell-making wizards have all
made their homes ?

I'm going to find it, perhaps
it's not far,
So start up the engines and head
for that star.

Count-down

Ten, nine, eight,
Rocket won't wait.
Eight, seven, six,
Time clock clicks.
Six, five, four,
Engines roar.
Four, three, two,
Count-down's through.
Two, one, zero,
And OFF WE GO!

Space Talk

CHUNK, CHUNK, BLEEP,
BLEEP.

What can I say ? What can I do ?
I'd like so much to talk to you.

BLIP, BLIP, BOING, BOING.

What can I do ? What can I say ?
When I've just come from Earth
today ?

KER-CHINK, KER-CHINK,
BIP, BIP.

What do you mean ?
                    Oh please don't go —
There's such a lot I want to know.

U.F.O.

Hear that humming . . .
Spaceship's coming.

Watch that light . . .
It's shining bright.

Feel that air . . .
It's landing there.

Hear that roar . . .
Look at the door.

See the crew . . .
They're coming through !

Time Trip

Can you imagine how it would be
To leave the house when you've
eaten your tea,
Climb in your time-ship and blast
off to see
How people lived in 10,000 B.C?

Or how the world looked when the
Pterosaurs flew
And the Earth was much hotter
and swampier too?

But, after all that, I'm sure
you'd be glad
To zoom home to supper with
mother and dad.

Twinkle, Twinkle, Little Star

Twinkle, Twinkle, I'm a star,
Are you a spaceman going far?
Will you explore the Milky Way?
Perhaps you'll visit me one day.

Time Machine

If ever you should want to go
Into the future, let me know.
My new machine can carry you
Forward to 1992.

You'd really like to try today ?
No time like now, I always say.
We'll get inside and shut the door,
I'll show you what the knobs are for.

Now please don't touch the one that's
                    red.
Just use the blue and green instead.
The green one first and then the blue,
You'll soon see what you have to do.

You must have heard me when I said
That you must NEVER touch the red.
Oh dear ! Oh dear ! Look what you've
                    done—
We're back in 1621.

The Message

A rocket pilot
Called from space
Hey, you on Earth,
I've found a place
Where there's a different
Kind of race.

They don't eat meat—
Just milk and honey.
They never work
And don't use money.
They sit about
For hours and hours
Just making garlands
Out of flowers.

Dear Mother . . .

Here is the photo
That I promised you
Of me in my spacesuit
With one of the crew.
This is the landing
I made with old Jim,
You'll recognise me,
The other one's him.

Mission Great Bear

This is Mission Great Bear,
        Mission Great Bear,
Guess what we found when we got
            there—
Machine men that talk,
Machine men that walk,
And little red hover-cars everywhere.

Kent's Flight

I used to know a boy called Kent,
So mad on rockets that he went
And hid in one at dead of night,
The day before it went in flight.

The rocket left on probe unmanned —
Except for Kent who wasn't planned!